# Titles in the series...

**Graphic Chillers**

## DRACULA

Bram Stoker • Daniel Conner • Rod Espinosa

**Graphic Chillers**

## FRANKENSTEIN

Mary Shelley • Elizabeth Genco • Jason Ho

**Graphic Chillers**

## THE INVISIBLE MAN

H.G. Wells • Joeming Dunn • Ben Dunn

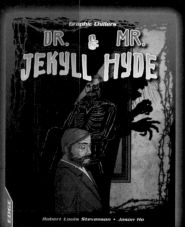

**Graphic Chillers**

## DR. & MR. JEKYLL HYDE

Robert Louis Stevenson • Jason Ho

**Graphic Chillers**

## THE LEGEND OF SLEEPY HOLLOW

Washington Irving • Jeff Zornow

**Graphic Chillers**

## MUMMY

Bram Stoker • Bart A. Thompson • Brian Miroglio

**Graphic Chillers**

## THE PHANTOM OF THE OPERA

Gaston Leroux • Joeming Dunn • Rod Espinosa

**Graphic Chillers**

## WEREWOLF

Jeff Zornow

# THE INVISIBLE MAN

## ABOUT THE AUTHOR

Herbert George Wells was born in Bromley, England, on 21 September, 1866. His father was a shopkeeper and his mother was a housekeeper. Wells attended Morley's School in Bromley, but did not learn much there. His real education came from reading on his own. At the age of 14, Wells was apprenticed to a draper but was soon dismissed. He then did several jobs before becoming an assistant in a grammar school.

At the age of 18, he won a scholarship to the Royal College of Science. He graduated from London University in 1888 and began teaching. Wells had always been interested in science fiction and soon he began writing his own work.

In 1895, Wells included the idea of time as the fourth dimension in his book *The Time Machine*. This concept was not discussed or accepted until 1905, when Albert Einstein published his work on the relativity of time.

Wells died on 13 August, 1946, in London. During his lifetime he wrote many successful non-fiction works. However, it is through his great science fiction works that he is best remembered.

*Graphic Chillers*

# THE INVISIBLE MAN

ADAPTED BY

## JOEMING DUNN

ILLUSTRATED BY

## BEN DUNN

BASED UPON THE WORKS OF

## H.G. WELLS

EDGE · FRANKLIN WATTS

LONDON·SYDNEY

# THE INVISIBLE MAN

ON A SNOWY DAY IN FEBRUARY, A STRANGER ENTERED THE VILLAGE OF IPING, ENGLAND.

Coach and Horses Inn

Welcome to Iping

IF YOU HELP ME, I WILL REWARD YOU. BUT IF YOU SHOULD BETRAY ME...

WHATEVER YOU WISH I AM WILLING TO DO.

FOR THE NEXT TWO DAYS, THOMAS ASSISTED THE INVISIBLE MAN.

THOMAS SOON WANTED HIS FREEDOM BACK. AS THE INVISIBLE MAN SLEPT, THOMAS RAN FOR THE NEAREST TOWN, PORT BURDOCK.

THE INVISIBLE MAN IS COMING!

HE'S COMING AFTER ME! YOU HAVE TO HIDE ME FROM HIM.

WHAT ARE YOU TALKING ABOUT?

THE INVISIBLE MAN! HE'S MAD, I TELL YOU! LOCK THE DOORS.

YOU CAN HIDE BEHIND HERE.

I HEARD ABOUT THIS INVISIBLE MAN FROM SOME PEOPLE IN IPING.

WE'LL BE READY TO DEAL WITH HIM.

WHAT'S THIS?

AS HE APPROACHED HIS BEDROOM DOOR, HE NOTICED SOMETHING WAS DIFFERENT...

THERE IS BLOOD ON THE HANDLE!

THE INVISIBLE MAN?

YES, DR. KEMP, IT'S ME.

IS THIS SOME... SOME SORT OF TRICK?

PLEASE TEND TO MY WOUND, MY GOOD DOCTOR.

"NOW, WITH MY NEW ABILITY, I COULD DO AS I PLEASED. I STOLE MONEY AT WILL, I ATE WHENEVER I WISHED, AND I STAYED WHEREVER I WANTED."

"BUT TO RETAIN MY ADVANTAGE, I HAD TO EXPOSE MY BODY TO THE ELEMENTS. I WAS FORCED TO GO ABOUT WITHOUT PROTECTION."

"THE RAIN OR SNOW MADE ME SHOW UP AS A WATERY OUTLINE."

"KNOWING I COULD NOT SURVIVE IN THE ELEMENTS FOR LONG, I STOLE A MASK FROM A COSTUME SHOP."

"THEN, I STOLE SOME CLOTHES."

"I COULD NOT WANDER THE STREETS WITHOUT NOTICE. BUT, I COULD NOT EAT PROPERLY WITH THE MASK ON."

"I STARTED TO WRAP MYSELF IN BANDAGES. I CAME UP WITH AN ELABORATE STORY ABOUT A CHEMICAL ACCIDENT."

This edition first published in 2010 by
Franklin Watts
338 Euston Road
London NW1 3BH

Franklin Watts Australia
Level 17/207 Kent Street
Sydney NSW 2000

First published in the USA by Magic Wagon, a division of the ABDO Group

1 3 5 7 9 10 8 6 4 2

Original novel by H.G. Wells
Adapted and lettered by Joeming Dunn
Illustrated by Ben Dunn
Coloured by Robby Bevard and Lee Duhig
Edited by Stephanie Hedlund and Rochelle Baltzer
Interior layout and design by Antarctic Press
Cover art by Ben Dunn
Original cover design by Neil Klinepier
UK cover design by Peter Scoulding

A CIP catalogue record for this book is available from the British Library.

Dewey number: 741.5

ISBN: 978 0 7496 9681 8

Printed in China

Franklin Watts is a division of Hachette Children's Books,
an Hachette UK company.
www.hachette.co.uk

# Graphic Chillers Sneak peak...

READ THE REST OF THIS STORY IN: DRACULA